Market Day

Heather Amery

Illustrated by Stephen Cartwright

Language consultant: Betty Root
Series editor: Jenny Tyler

There is a little yellow duck to find on every page.

This is Apple Tree Farm.

This is Mrs. Boot, the farmer. She has two children, called Poppy and Sam, and a dog called Rusty.

Today is market day.

Mrs. Boot puts the trailer on the car. Poppy and
Sam put a wire crate in the trailer.

They drive to the market.

Mrs. Boot, Poppy and Sam walk past cows, sheep and pigs. They go to the shed which has cages of birds.

There are different kinds of geese.

"Let's look in all the cages," says Mrs. Boot.
"I want four nice young geese."

"There are four nice white ones."

"They look nice and friendly," says Poppy.
"Yes, they are just what I want," says Mrs. Boot.

A woman is selling the geese.

"How much are the four white ones?" asks Mrs. Boot. "I'll buy them, please." She pays for them.

"We'll come back later."

"Let's look at the other birds," says Sam. There are cages with hens, chicks, ducks and pigeons.

"Look at the poor little duck."

"It's lonely," says Poppy. "Please may I buy it?
I can pay for it with my own money."

"Yes, you can buy it."

"We'll get it when we come back for the geese,"
says Mrs. Boot. Poppy pays the man for the duck.

Mrs. Boot brings the crate.

Poppy opens the lid. The woman passes the geese to Mrs. Boot. She puts them in the crate.

One of the geese runs away.

A goose jumps out of the crate just before Sam
shuts the door. It runs very fast out of the shed.

"Catch that goose."

Mrs. Boot, Poppy and Sam run after the goose.
The goose jumps through an open car door.

"Now we've got it," says Sam.

But a woman opens a door on the other side.
The goose jumps out of the car and runs away.

"Run after it," says Mrs. Boot.

The goose runs into the plant tent.
"There it is," says Sam, and picks it up.

"Let's go home," says Mrs. Boot.

"I've got my geese now." "And I've got my duck," says Poppy. "Markets are fun," says Sam.

Cover design by Hannah Ahmed   Digital manipulation by Sarah Cronin
This edition first published in 2004 by Usborne Publishing Ltd, 83-85 Saffron Hill, London EC1N 8RT, England. www.usborne.com